The Garden of Time

Jill Hammer
Art by Zoë Cohen

Skinner House Books
Boston

For our children: Raya, Naftali, and Nomi

www.skinnerhouse.org

Printed in the United States

ISBN: 978-1-55896-729-8

6 5 4 3 2 1
16 15 14

Library of Congress Cataloging-in-Publication Data

Hammer, Jill.
The garden of time / by Jill Hammer ; Illustrated by Zoë Cohen.
    pages cm
ISBN 978-1-55896-729-8 (hardcover : alk. paper) 1. Fasts and feasts—Judaism—
Juvenile literature. I. Cohen, Zoë, illustrator. II. Title.
  BM690.H2538 2014
  296.4'3—dc23
                        2013037165

Foreword

To everything there is a season and a time for every purpose under heaven.

—Ecclesiastes 3

It is the moon that determines the cycle of the months and the sun that tells us the rhythm of the year. Regardless of human invention, to everything there is a season. The harvest of autumn, the frozen winter, the birth of spring, and the fullness of summer come and go, determined solely by the earth's revolutions. It matters not to the earth if there are human witnesses.

It is the imagination of human beings that gives meaning to the planet's orbit. We are the ones who divide the months into weeks, the year into sacred moments, occasions for rest and commemoration. We give labels to the divisions of time, calling days by name and measuring the years.

As the wind blows warm and cold, around and within us, we give meaning to time. *The Garden of Time* is a gentle teacher of the purpose the Jewish people assign to the changing seasons. From the first autumn breezes that mark a New Year to the hot humid summer days that embrace revelation, loss, and love, the calendar invites us to match the cycles of our personal and communal lives with nature's turnings.

The themes of sacred times are tied not only to agricultural cycles but to the passages of the human spirit.

We begin the New Year not in the spring with beginnings, as we might have expected, but in the autumn with regeneration. We approach each new counting of time with forgiveness and renewal. The human heart knows that to begin is not as difficult as to begin again.

As the leaves turn to even brighter oranges and reds and the harvest is full and ripe, we offer thanks. When the rains begin to fall and the nights turn chilly, we might expect to express dread at the unknown winter to come. Instead, we express gratitude. That, as much as a rich harvest, sustains us through frosty months ahead. When the days are shortest, we light candles, not with magic's spark but with flashes of courage and hope. Despair gives way to trust in another season, another promise.

Spring returns, with or without our believing that it will. Once again the human heart opens freely in trust, wiser from a year's journey. The breath of life knows sadness and love, loss and renewal. And so, as the leaves fall another time, we are taught how to begin – again.

With beautiful images and words, *The Garden of Time* offers a magical path through the seasons and allows the sacred breath of life to blow through all our souls. Take a walk in the garden; be refreshed and renewed.

—Sandy Eisenberg Sasso
author, *Midrash: Reading the Bible with Question Marks*

The Holy One passed through the year, and then passed those teachings on to Adam in the garden of Eden . . . and Eve taught these things to her great-grandson Enoch. . . .
— Pirkei de Rabbi Eliezer
an eighth-century Jewish book of legends

This story is set in the Garden of Eden. It is based on a Jewish legend in which God teaches Adam and Eve about the days, nights, months, and seasons. God also teaches the first people the Jewish calendar, with all of its holidays, before sending them out into the world. Adam and Eve pass down all this wisdom about time to their children and their children's children.

   We invite you to use this book to teach yourself and your children about the Jewish holidays and the ways that these holidays teach wonder at the beauty of nature, tell ancient stories, and express gratitude for the meaning in our lives. No matter what religion you practice, or how you relate to spirituality, this book may offer some insight into the ways that the seasons of the year can show us how to live.

   In this book, the wind stands in for the character of God in Genesis. A biblical verse says, "A wind of God was sweeping over the water, and God said, 'Let there be light.'" Depending on your own belief, you can explain the wind in this book as God, as nature, as the spirit of life in all things, as the voice of human wisdom, or as a character in the story who helps the people find their way through the garden of time.

   There are guides to the holidays and to the iconography used in the art at the back of the book. The origins of Jewish holidays arise from historical events and legends as well as shifts in the seasons, and you can learn more about them in the notes to the book. We hope you will enjoy and learn from this journey through the seasons.

A man and a woman slept on the warm earth. They did not have names yet. The wind flowed over their faces and touched their cheeks and eyelids. The wind breathed the breath of life into them, and they woke up into the bright sun. With their first breath, time began.

The woman and the man stood up on the earth out of
which they had been born. Around them was a garden
of fruit trees and blossoming vines. The sun and moon
in the sky danced for them. The vines sent forth grapes
for them. The trees grew figs for them. The wind made
music in the leaves.

Then the wind blew into their ears and said, "This is Eden, the garden of time. In it are the tree of life and the tree of unfolding days. Come, follow me down the paths of the months, and walk on the hills of the seasons. See how the sun rises and sets, and how the moon changes in the sky."

"See how the light grows and fades and grows again, from one day to the next," the wind said. "See how each season has colors, smells, and tastes. Every moment has a blessing to give." The woman and the man set off down the path, to find the gifts of the days and the seasons.

The path led to autumn. Pomegranates, pumpkins, and apples shone. Rain glittered in the sky. "Feel the sweetness in the earth," whispered the wind. "Feel the sorrow of the falling leaves. This is the beginning of the world, the time to remember, learn, and start again. Name these days Rosh haShanah, head of the year, and Yom Kippur, time of returning."

"Next year, sweet apples and pomegranates will remind us of our blessings," said the man. "We will look into our hearts, and be grateful for what we have." "The new year will be our birthday, and make us new," said the woman. "Let us save the seeds of the fruit, so that we can plant again."

The wind urged them on a little further. Over the next hill was a starry night. "See the stars," cried the wind. "Touch the strength of the tall trees. Look up at the night sky, and feel beneath you the goodness of earth. Name these days Sukkot, the festival of dwelling in beauty."

The man looked up at the evening sky. "Next year," said the man to the woman, "let us build a roofless house, so that we can see the stars." The woman replied, "Let us lay branches over the open roof and smell their fragrance, and bring earth and sky together." The people saw that autumn was good.

"Come down the path to winter," the wind called. The
man and the woman walked into rain and snow. Days
grew shorter, and nights grew longer. Then the path
turned, and the winter nights grew shorter again.
"Celebrate the return of the sun's warmth," the wind
sang. "Feel courage and hope stirring within you.
Name these days Chanukah, the festival of light."

The woman saw an olive tree growing in the earth.
She plucked an olive. "Next year," she said, "let us pick
olives when the winter comes, and shape our lamps to
be like trees." The man said, "We'll use the olive oil to
fill the lamps, and we will kindle fire to welcome the
longer days."

The wind guided them to a snowy meadow. In one field, the trees were bare, but in another, almond trees were bursting into bloom. "See the world waking up," smiled the wind. "Sap is rising in the trees, and blossoms appear on earth. Name this day Tu b'Shevat, the festival of trees."

The man sniffed the wind and said, "Next year, let us celebrate the buds and the rising sap." The woman said, "Let's eat many kinds of fruit, to remember how good the trees are to us." The people saw that the winter was good.

The wind called, and the people followed. On a
frozen river, the ice cracked. Bears woke up. Crocuses
bloomed. The people found themselves laughing and
singing. "Spring rescues everyone from winter," the
wind shouted happily, "and chases away the cold and
ice. The spring brings breezes of change. Name this
day Purim, the festival of good luck."

The man and the woman watched as new lambs were born, and their hearts were happy. "Next year at this time, let us sing and laugh and tell stories," they said. "Let us wear masks and turn ourselves into many creatures, and remember how all things can change." The people saw that the spring was good.

Then the wind blew toward golden barley, and whispered sadly, "One day, some people will enslave others. But the wind will pass over and free them. Name these days Pesach, the festival of passing over." "Next year," said the man, "let us tell the story of freedom." The woman said, "Let us eat flat bread, for we are free as wild grain."

The people climbed hills of wheat. "Cut grain. Pick
fruit," the wind thundered. "One day at this season,
I will teach you how to live. Call these days Shavuot,
the festival of growing." The woman said, "Next year,
let us offer our first fruits in thanks." The man added,
"And celebrate the gift of wisdom, which teaches us to
be grateful."

The path led to summer. Roses lost petals. Plants wilted. The wind murmured, "This is the time to grieve. One day at this season, the people will remember a beloved home they lost. Name this day Tisha b'Av, the day to remember. A few days later, celebrate Tu b'Av, the day of love, and all the good things to come."

Figs and grapes ripened and fell. Lambs grew older.
"Next year," said the man, "we will reflect on our
first days in Eden and long for the past." "Next year,"
said the woman, "we will dance in the vineyards and
celebrate the ripening of the future." The people saw
that the summer was good.

The wind blew down the path, and the people found themselves in autumn again. "Now," the wind whispered, "you must leave Eden, but you will live in the garden of time all the days of your lives. You are part of the seasons. Tend them carefully, and enjoy their fruits."

"How will we find our way through the years without you?" the woman asked. The wind replied, "I am the breath of life. I am in all times and places. I will be with you in every season."

The man asked, "How will we know when to celebrate the special days that you have given to us? What if we forget how to know the seasons?"

The wind replied, "The moon will show you when the months begin and when the festivals fall. The sun will guide you through the days and seasons. If you forget anything that I have told you, the great lights in the sky will remind you."

Gently, the wind blew the people into the world. They
harvested and planted. They found themselves names:
Adam, which means earth, and Eve, which means life.
Always, there was a circle of sun and rain, night and
day, seed and fruit, earth and sky. Always, the wind
was with them to blow them toward the next season.

From the first people came many new people. They too came to know the garden of time and love its paths and seasons. They too celebrated the festivals of the autumn and spring, of cold winter and warm, wild summer. Many years later, we are all still living in the garden of time.

NOTES

In the book of Genesis, a man and woman named Adam and Eve are the first human beings. They live in the garden of Eden. One Jewish legend (Babylonian Talmud, Rosh haShanah 27a) tells that the first people are created in the autumn, at the season of harvest. Another legend (Pirkei de Rabbi Eliezer 7) says that God taught Adam and Eve the calendar so that they could teach it to their children.

Rosh haShanah, the Jewish new year, falls in the autumn at the new moon. Apples are a traditional Rosh haShanah food: they are eaten with honey as a wish that the coming year will be sweet. Pomegranate seeds represent the good deeds we hope to do in the coming year. **Yom Kippur**, the day of atonement, comes right after Rosh haShanah. It is a time for remembering our better selves and turning back to the right path.

Jews celebrate the autumn harvest holiday of **Sukkot** (the feast of Tabernacles) at the full moon. They build temporary huts covered in greens, partly open to the sky so that the people inside can see the stars. For a week, people eat and sleep inside the huts, experiencing the beauty and vulnerability of nature as their ancestors did during the harvest season.

The holiday of **Chanukah**, which falls around the time of the winter solstice, commemorates the Maccabean victory over the ancient Seleucid Empire. As a result of this victory, the Jewish temple was re-dedicated. According to a legend, only one jar of oil was left to light the menorah (the Temple lamp) and the oil miraculously lasted eight days. This holiday expresses our gratitude for the miracle of light at the darkest time of year. Olive oil is used to light Chanukah lamps and to fry latkes (potato pancakes) and doughnuts.

Tu b'Shevat, which means "the fifteenth of the month of Shevat," is the Jewish festival of the trees. In the land of Israel, almond trees bloom at this time. In temperate climates in the Northern Hemisphere, Tu b'Shevat comes as the sap is beginning to rise. Some Jews later developed a mystical tradition of commemorating the day by eating many kinds of fruits and reciting prayers blessing nature.

The holiday of **Purim**, when Jews tell the biblical story of Queen Esther, comes in late winter. In the story of Queen Esther, a Jewish girl becomes queen of Persia. When the king's evil advisor seeks to destroy the Jews, Esther chooses to risk her life and implore the king to save her people. The story lends itself to costumes and drama, and since the Middle Ages, Purim is celebrated with joy, masks, costumes, plays, frivolity, and jokes. Purim is similar to other spring holidays around the world, like Mardi Gras, where rules are loosened and people act in wild and silly ways.

Passover, which may have its origins as a feast of the barley harvest, is the Jewish festival of freedom, recalling the story in Exodus about how the Hebrew slaves left Egypt. Passover involves the eating of unleavened bread and the telling of how God redeemed the Hebrews from slavery and led them through the Sea of Reeds into the wilderness. Seven weeks later, Jews celebrate **Shavuot**, the festival of the wheat harvest (also known as Pentecost). Jewish legend associates Shavuot with the story of how the Jews received the Torah at Mt. Sinai, and the Shavuot holiday includes a celebration of the giving of the Torah. These holidays were once pilgrimage festivals when farmers made gifts of grain and other growing things to the Temple and to the poor.

In the summer, Jews observe the fast of **Tisha b'Av** (the ninth of Av), remembering the date when, according to tradition, their Temples were destroyed. The Babylonians destroyed the First Temple in the sixth century B.C.E. and the Romans destroyed the Second Temple in the first century C.E. It has become a day of universal mourning for tragedies that have befallen the Jewish people. A week later, there is a little-known ancient holiday called **Tu b'Av**, the grape harvest festival. Long ago, in the land of Israel, girls would dress in white and go out to dance in the vineyards in order to celebrate the harvest. Tu b'Av is the end of the sad time of Tisha b'Av and the beginning of the joyful new year season.

Jewish legend says that Adam and Eve left Eden in autumn, at the time of the Jewish new year. The Jewish calendar begins in autumn, and each Jewish holiday falls in a season that expresses that holiday's spirit. But no matter what calendar we use, we are celebrating the beauty of creation as it changes with the seasons.

GUIDE TO ICONOGRAPHY

The illustrations in this book are partly based on visual research into the belief systems and art of the Ancient Near East. While much of the art is from my imagination, I tried to create the images with a visual style inspired by my source materials. Some symbols used in the book, listed below, are drawn directly from Ancient Near Eastern art from Canaanite, Assyrian, Ugaritic, Mesopotamian, Babylonian, and Sumerian cultures that existed just prior to, or at the same time as, early Hebraic culture. —Zoë Cohen

The First Humans

The human figures in this book are based on a Neo-Assyrian ivory inlay relief carving of a male figure holding a vine, from the eighth century BCE. Assyrian artists often depicted people in profile in their relief carvings, with prominent facial features.

The Sun

A few different symbols are used to depict the sun in this book. The sun with alternating long pointed rays and rounded "petals" is based on a Babylonian relief carving of the Sun God, Shamash. The sun as a "Winged Disc" is a symbol that originated in ancient Egypt and then spread to Mesopotamia and the Levant, and then appeared on Hebrew seals around the eighth century BCE.

The Wind and Weather

The spiraling pattern used to depict weather, and the voice of the wind, is a commonly found linear pattern from Ancient Near Eastern art. I first came across it in an image of a fragment of Coptic (Christian Egyptian) textile.

The Sacred Bull

The bull peering out from the undergrowth is based on a restored Iranian stone sculpture from Persepolis from around 450 BCE. In Mesopotamian mythology, the bull was associated with lunar qualities, its horns representing the crescent phase of the moon.

Other imagery in this book based on Ancient Near Eastern visual sources includes the green grasses and date palms, and the grains.